Upstairs Mouse, Downstairs MOLE

BY WONG HERBERT YEE

Houghton Mifflin Company
Boston

www.houghtonmifflinbooks.com

The text of this book is set in Adobe Caslon.
The illustrations are bamboo pen and watercolor with colored pencil.

Library of Congress Cataloging-in-Publication Data
Yee, Wong Herbert.
Upstairs Mouse, downstairs Mole / by Wong Herbert Yee.
p. cm.
Summary: Mouse and her downstairs neighbor, Mole, discover that when
they help each other, housecleaning and other daily tasks are much easier.
PA ISBN-13 978-0-618-91586-6
HC ISBN-13: 978-0-618-47313-7
[1. Mice—Fiction. 2. Moles (Animals)—Fiction. 3. Neighborliness—
Fiction. 4. Cooperativeness—Fiction. 5. Cleanliness—Fiction.] I. Title.
PZ7.Y3655Up 2005
[Fic]—dc22   2004005238

Printed in Singapore
TWP 10 9 8 7 6 5 4 3 2

For Friends of Frog and Toad

CONTENTS

Clean and TIDY

Mouse and Mole are neighbors.

Mouse lives in a house inside an oak tree.

Mole lives in a hole under the house of Mouse.

Every morning, Mole swept his hole.

Sweep—sweep—sweep!

Mole liked his hole nice and tidy.

Every evening, Mouse swept *her* house.

Sweep—sweep—sweep!

Mouse kept her house nice and clean.

But when Mouse swept her house,
the dirt went below into Mole's hole.
This made Mole angry.

He knocked on
Mouse's door:
TAP-TAP-TAP.

"Evening, Mole," said Mouse.

"Evening, Mouse," said Mole.

"Did you know that when
you sweep, all *your* dirt
goes down into *my* hole?
I sweep my place nice and tidy
in the morning, but by evening,
it needs to be swept all over again!"

"If you sweep in the morning,"
said Mouse, "and then again
in the evening . . .

Why, you have *twice* as much
work as I do. That does not
seem fair." Together, they
sat down on the stoop.
Mouse twirled her tail.
Mole rubbed his snout.

"I have an idea!" squeaked Mouse. She told
Mole her new plan. They shook paws.
"Good night," said
Mouse to Mole.
"Good night," said
Mole to Mouse.

The next morning when Mole woke up,
he did not sweep his hole.

At twelve o'clock sharp, he grabbed his broom
and knocked on Mouse's door: TAP-TAP-TAP.

"Good afternoon," said Mole to Mouse.

"Good afternoon," said Mouse to Mole.

Mouse ran to fetch *her* broom.

Together, they swept Mouse's house

until it was nice and clean.

"Why, it only took us *half* the time it takes me to sweep my house," said Mouse. Next they marched downstairs and swept Mole's hole until it was nice and tidy. Together it had taken less time to sweep *both* places than it took for each of them to do just one.

"That was fast," said Mole. "Our houses are clean *and* tidy, thanks to you. Now what?"

"I've been thinking of a garden," said Mouse.

Outside, Mouse and Mole circled the tree.

Mole rubbed his snout.

"Where should we put it?"

"How about in back?" said Mouse,

twirling her tail. "Then we

will have a backyard."

"Good thinking!"

exclaimed Mole.

First, they dug up a patch of grass.

Next, they raked the dirt until it was soft.

Mole dug a row of holes. Mouse dropped a seed
into each one. Then it was Mouse's turn to dig,
and Mole's to plant. Back and forth they went
until the garden was finished.

"Whew!" said Mole. "That was hard work!"

"But only *half* as hard, thanks to you,"
said Mouse.

They decided to take a nap.

Mole went down into his hole.

Mouse went inside her house.

Both were much too tired to bother
with the dirt they tracked into
their clean and tidy homes.

The INVITATIONS

Mouse found an invitation in her mailbox.
It was from her neighbor, Mole.

Dear Mouse,
If you are not too busy,
please come join me for
lunch to celebrate our
new garden.

Your neighbor
(downstairs),
Mole

Around noon there came a TAP-TAP-TAP
at Mole's door. "Glad you could make it,"
said Mole. "Please come in!"

Mouse had picked dandelions for the occasion.
"For you," she said, "until our flowers come up."
Mouse looked around the room. "My, but you
keep a nice tidy hole," she squeaked.
"Thank you!" said Mole.

It was a bit damp
inside Mole's hole.
Mouse shivered.

Mole also kept his place rather dark,
as bright lights hurt his eyes.
Mouse bumped into the table as she sat down.

Mole poured a cup of tea for Mouse
and one for himself. "I wasn't sure how you
liked your worms," said Mole, "so I prepared
them *two* ways. The ones on the right
are lightly fried. The ones on the left
have not been cooked. Dig in!"

Mouse took one of each
to be polite.

Mole filled his plate. He was starved!

Mole crunched, Mole slurped.

Mouse poked the worms on her plate.

The one on the left wiggled and squirmed.

Mouse's stomach began to wiggle and squirm.

The one on the right looked greenish gray.

Mouse's face turned a greenish gray.

The damp air made
her sneeze—*ACHOO!*

"Goodness, Mouse!" said Mole.

"You do not look well."

"I don't feel so good," moaned Mouse.

"Please excuse me, Mole, but I think

I had better go upstairs and lie down."

She bumped into the door on her way out.

That evening, Mole found an invitation
in *his* mailbox.

Dear Mole,
I am feeling much
better. Please join
me for dinner at
six o'clock to continue
our garden celebration.

Your neighbor
(upstairs),

Mouse

At six o'clock there came a

TAP-TAP-TAP at Mouse's door.

"Right on time," said Mouse.

"Please come in!"

"You are looking much better," said Mole.

"Thank you!" said Mouse.

The evening sun poured through the windows

in Mouse's house. Mole covered his eyes.

He walked *smack* into a wall.

Mole bumped into the table as he sat down.

Mouse poured a cup of tea for Mole
and one for herself.

"I was not sure which cheese you preferred," said Mouse, "so I cut up *two* kinds. The one on the left is cheddar, and the one on the right is Limburger. Help yourself!"

To be polite, Mole took a thin slice of each.
Mouse loaded her plate.
She was famished.
Mouse nibbled,
Mouse gnawed.

Mole's head still ached from walking
into the wall. He began to wobble in his seat.

The bright light over the table hurt his eyes.

The strong odor of Limburger

made his stomach flip-flop.

PLOP! Mole toppled right off the chair.

"Mercy, Mole!" squeaked Mouse.

"Are you okay?"

Mole groaned. "I feel a bit dizzy.

Please excuse me, Mouse, but I think

I had better go downstairs and rest."

He bumped into the door

on his way out.

Kind, Good NEIGHBORS

Mole woke up the next morning feeling
refreshed. He looked around his tidy hole.
How nicely dark and damp it was—nothing like
Mouse's house, which was warm and bright.

Suddenly, Mole pictured
Mouse shivering.
He remembered
Mouse sneezing,
Mouse bumping
into the table, and
Mouse smacking into
the door. Why, Mouse had not
even touched the worms on her plate!
"Goodness!" cried Mole. "How selfish of me!"
He buttoned his jacket and rushed out the door.

Mouse washed the dishes in the sink.

Rays of sunshine streamed into the kitchen.

How bright and cheery things looked—

not at all like Mole's dark hole.

Suddenly, Mouse pictured Mole

covering his eyes.

She remembered Mole
walking into the wall,
Mole falling off his chair,
and Mole bumping
into the door. Why,
Mole had not even
nibbled the cheese
on his plate.

"Mercy me!" squeaked Mouse.

"What a thoughtless neighbor I've been!"

She zipped her coat and raced out the door.

Mouse tied a bow
on her box and
hurried downstairs.
Mole finished
wrapping his package.
He went upstairs
to call on Mouse.

They bumped into each other outside.

"Why, hello!" said Mouse to Mole.

"Hello!" said Mole to Mouse.

"This is for you," said Mole. "I hope you
don't think me a thoughtless neighbor."

Mouse opened the present.

There were two candles inside the box.

"Bring them when you visit," said Mole,
"and my hole will be less dark and damp."

"Thank you very much," said Mouse.

"You are a *kind* neighbor, Mole."

Mouse handed Mole her box.

"I hope *I* haven't been too selfish a neighbor."

Mole unwrapped the package.

Inside was a pair of sunglasses.

"Wear them when you visit," said Mouse,

"and my house will not seem so bright."

"Thank *you* very much!" said Mole.

"You are a *good* neighbor, Mouse."

Together, they strolled into town for dessert.
Mouse had the cheesecake. As for Mole,
a bowl of worms—lightly fried.

The BOAT

Mole knocked on Mouse's door: TAP-TAP-TAP.

"Good morning, Mole," said Mouse.

"Good morning, Mouse," said Mole.

"I hope you like surprises."

"I love surprises!" squeaked Mouse.

"Don't tell. Let me try to guess."

"It has to do with water," whispered Mole.

Mouse twirled her tail. It had not rained in two days. The flowers in the garden were starting to droop.

She hopped up
and down on one foot.
"Is it a rain dance?" guessed Mouse.

"Nope," said Mole, "not a rain dance."
Mouse waved her arms back and forth
as if she were casting a line.

"Are we going fishing, then?"
"No, not fishing either," said Mole.
Mouse scratched her ears. She was hot
from hopping up and down. Her arms
were tired from waving back and forth.
"Swimming?" she squeaked hopefully.

"Wrong again!" said Mole. "Follow me."

They hiked along the path to the pond.

There in the water was a boat.

"SURPRISE!" shouted Mole.

"My, what a *beautiful* boat!" said Mouse.

"I have only one paddle, though," said Mole.

"No problem," said Mouse. "We'll take turns."

"Good thinking." Mole smiled.

Off they went.

Mole paddled and paddled.

Then he paddled some more.

His arms were getting sore.

They had passed the willow tree *three* times.

"I think we are going in circles,"
said Mouse. "Here, let me try."
Mouse paddled and paddled.

Then she paddled some more.
Soon Mouse's arms began to ache.

They passed the willow tree three more times;
only now they were headed in the *opposite*
direction. "You're right, Mouse," said Mole.
"We are *definitely* going in circles!"
Both Mouse and Mole were hot
and tired from all the paddling.
"Let's go for a swim,"
suggested Mole.
They dove into the water.
Mouse splished!
Mole splashed!
How refreshing!

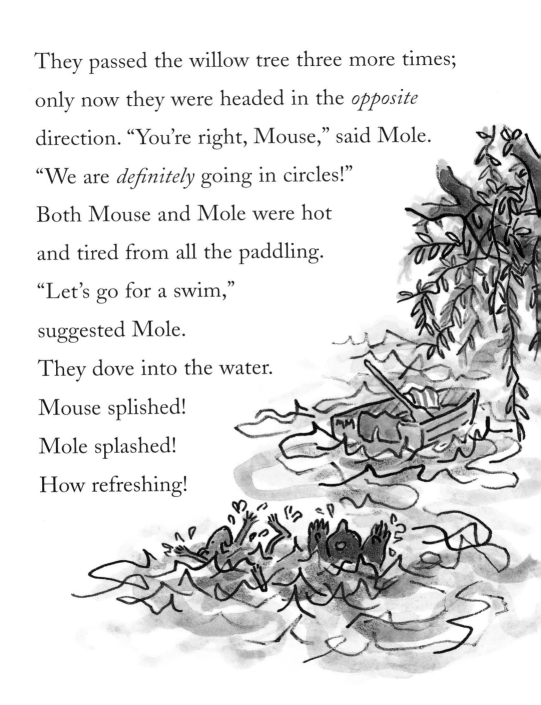

They climbed back into the boat.

Mouse twirled her tail.

Mole rubbed his snout.

"I have an idea!" squeaked Mouse.

"Why not switch paddling more often?"

"Good thinking." Mole chuckled.

"At least we won't tire as easily."

Pretty soon Mouse and Mole were zipping across the pond. When they reached the other side, it was time to turn around. Mouse and Mole were *experts* at turning around!

"Ouch!" squeaked Mouse.
"Something is nibbling
on my tail!" She yanked it
out of the water. A fish
flopped into the boat.
"Way to go!" said Mole.
"Our first fish!"

Mouse and Mole hopped up and down in
celebration. They waved their arms back and
forth at the sky. Then it began to rain!

The next day, Mouse knocked on

Mole's door: TAP-TAP-TAP.

"I have a surprise for you," whispered Mouse.

"Let me guess!" Mole clapped.

Like Mouse, he too was fond of surprises.

"It has to do with pairs," she said.

"Do you mean *pears* like on a tree,"

asked Mole, "or *pairs* like mittens?"

"Like mittens," said Mouse,

"only *not* mittens."

Mole rubbed his snout.

He kicked the dirt with his feet.

A claw poked out of

one shoe. "Is it shoes

or socks?" guessed Mole.

"Nope, not shoes,

not socks," said Mouse.

She disappeared behind the tree.

"SURPRISE!" Out jumped Mouse. She handed
Mole a paddle decorated with ribbons.
"Now we have a pair of paddles!"
"A *pair* . . ." said Mole, "like *you* and *me*!"
Together, they hopped up and down,
dancing in circles around the oak tree.
Mole waved the paddle back and forth
at the sky. *Plip—PLOP!* Down came the rain
once again. Mouse and Mole's garden
never looked better!